After the Glass Slipper

♥

8 Proven Steps to Lasting Love

D0878251

Praise for
After the Glass Slipper

"Sheer genius! This is a delightful book. Perfect for after the honeymoon as reality sinks in."
– Diane Sollee
Founder and Director, Smart Marriages

"Enchanting! So much on target. I use the book regularly in counseling couples along with *I and Thou* by Martin Buber and *The Art of Loving* by Erich Fromm."
– Rabbi Harold White
Senior Rabbi, Georgetown University

"Jon and Beverly Meyerson have distilled their years of experience into this wise and witty book."
– Steve Roberts
Co-author of the New York Times bestseller, *From This Day Forward.*

"*After The Glass Slipper* is a great book for newlyweds, and for those who aren't. After the honeymoon Fairy Godmother or Caring Godfather step in with excellent advice to help out the royal couple."
– Christina Lockstein,
Christy's Book Blog

"I had a warm, happy time reading *After the Glass Slipper*. It's wonderful seeing the Imago Therapy concepts showing up in this incredible follow-up to Cinderella!"
– Dorsey Cartwright
President, Austin, Texas Association for Marriage and Family Therapy

" I recommend this profound and magical book to all couples I marry and counsel."
– Rev. Susan Bierker
Sarasota, Florida

"I just finished your book and loved it. It is highly readable, humorous and chock full of good advice."
– Karen Koenig
Therapist and author of *The Rules of "Normal" Eating*

"Thank you for writing such a delightful and insightful book. As a marriage & family therapist, I really appreciated your insights. As a married man, I'm encouraged once again, to apply your insights to life! Thank you—thank you—thank you and God bless you!"
– Dr. Robb Palmer
Family therapist and Pastoral Counselor, Lebanon, Pennsylvania

National Healthy
Marriage Resource Center

After the Glass Slipper

(The Cinderella Story Mom Never Told You)

♥

8 Proven Steps To Lasting Love

Jon and Beverly Meyerson

Two Vus Press

Bethesda, Maryland • Sarasota, Florida

BOOK DESIGN: Barbara Shaw
COVER DESIGN: Susan Shapiro
COVER ART: Alberto Ruggieri/Getty Images

Library of Congress Control Number: 2007906520
ISBN: 978-0-9796983-2-3

Printed in the United States

Table of Contents

Preface

AFTER THE GLASS SLIPPER was written to introduce the eight essential skills in developing and keeping a loving relationship, and to provide an inspiring book to read while learning these skills. Although the book is written as fiction, each short chapter contains an important lesson. It expands on the world's best known fairy tale, *Cinderella*, describing what occurs after Cinderella and the Prince are married.

Romance and falling in love are part of the essence of being human. Most of us have experienced the ecstasy of falling in love. However, most romantic relationships enter a second phase of love: A power struggle ensues as conflicts arise and romance fades. Though we all wish to avoid this phase, it is another characteristic of being human.

Fortunately, we have an opportunity to enter a third phase of love, that of long-term, enduring love. In this phase we use conflict as a means toward healing and growth. Many couples never arrive at this stage since they have not been taught the skills. We have counseled hundreds of couples and found that almost all who have the desire, can learn these essential skills and experience the bliss of lasting love.

By following the path that Cinderella and the Prince take in *AFTER THE GLASS SLIPPER*, you, too, will be able to *live happily ever after.*

Jon & Beverly Meyerson

Acknowledgements

E ARE deeply thankful to our friends, family and colleagues who have supported us in writing this book. The wisdom of those who work with couples and write about couples' relationships has been invaluable. The comments and suggestions that our friends and relatives offered, have made *AFTER THE GLASS SLIPPER* a much better book.

Those whose ideas have been of special value are: Dottie and Hal Miller, Gruine Robinson, Noah Meyerson, Hester Grippando, Margaret Blair, Anita Thiel Winters, Marjory Goldman, Judy and Jonathan Knight, Ming and Tina Louie, Michael Andelson, Dorothy and Alan Somerville, Carol Hanlon, John Lindell, Laura and Stuart Mestelman, and Milton Cohen.

In addition, we are especially grateful to the hundreds of couples whom we have counseled, whose efforts to improve their relationships have been remarkable. They have provided us with vital information on what does or does not work in achieving lasting love.

Introduction

INDERELLA. The name alone evokes such romantic feelings! Countries and cultures around the world have embraced the Cinderella fairy tale.

Cinderella and the Prince (or simply, *Prince*, as he is known in this book) fell in love. We, too, have fallen in love and we, too, expected to *live happily ever after*. When we fell in love, the magical experience convinced us that our fairy godmother must have arranged it. And maybe she did. We had no doubt that the love we felt would endure forever and ever.

But in the months or years that passed, we often found that we weren't living happily ever after because our partner had changed dramatically.

Where was this person we first met? We knew him or her as our best friend who would make us happy, bring us joy, and be our true love. Where did our lover go? Why were we so easily fooled?

But we did not give up. We believed that we could recapture our love. We decided to mold our partner back into his or her *original* form. First, we tried gently. We suggested, we learned to sweet talk, we quietly explained, we coaxed.

That didn't work. So we offered long, detailed instructions, we cajoled, we pleaded, we demanded, and finally, we blamed. Over time we pushed harder and harder but found only deaf ears. Oddly, the more we tried, the less our partner resembled our original true love. Soon we found we were living with a stranger.

Now we wonder if our fairy godmother helped us select the wrong person. Maybe next time she will get it right! Next time, it will be the perfect match!

But if we ask her to find someone new, we may discover that history repeats itself. We will again find we have been fooled. Will it never end?

AFTER THE GLASS SLIPPER reveals how Cinderella and Prince learn to live happily ever after. The book continues the Cinderella tale from the moment her foot glides effortlessly into the glass slipper.

At first, the royal couple are deeply and blindly in love. However, they gradually experience the same conflicts that occur in all love relationships. They argue over values, such as how best to communicate with relatives. They don't believe their partner listens or understands them. They have conflicts over physical intimacy and disputes over ways to spend money.

But surprisingly, they are able to use each conflict to build a stronger and more loving relationship. How do they do this? Not alone, but with the help of their Fairy Godmother and Caring Godfather. Using the godparents' guidance, Cinderella and Prince become conscious of how they each generate conflict. By using special communication skills, the two of them can work together to recapture their feelings of love.

They learn to live happily ever after. You, too, can use these skills to live happily ever after with the love of your life!

The prince proclaimed that he would marry the woman whose foot fit into the glass slipper. For days his couriers tried to fit the slipper on all the ladies in the kingdom, but, alas, no one's foot would fit. Finally, they came upon the stepsisters' home and each sister tried to squeeze her foot into the slipper, to no avail. The courier was about to leave when he spied Cinderella in a back room. Though her stepsisters laughed at the idea that Cinderella should try on the glass slipper, the courier followed the prince's order to try the slipper on all young ladies in the kingdom. He found that Cinderella's foot fit as if it was made of wax. Further, Cinderella drew the matching slipper from her pocket and presented it to the courier.

— From *Cinderella*, Charles Perrault, 1697

I
The Royal Wedding

HE ROYAL WEDDING was held three weeks to the day after Cinderella's foot slipped perfectly into the glass slipper. Cinderella had a glorious time preparing for her nuptials with Prince. Her stepmother and stepsisters worked full time to assure that "our bride" would be appropriately prepared for the wedding.

Cinderella's stepsisters made many amends. She was no longer required to sleep on a sack of straw near the attic. Instead, her stepsisters vacated their sitting room, which became Cinderella's sleeping quarters. They sewed for days to prepare a lengthy bridal train. And what's more, her stepsisters and stepmother began to speak warmly to her, making her feel that she at last had a loving family. She also heard them chat with glee about joining the royal family.

All was not perfect. A week before the wedding, Cinderella's father posted a note on her chamber door:

My Dear Daughter:

Unfortunately, it will be impossible for me to partake in the merriment following your wedding ceremony. Several months ago I was favoured to receive an invitation to attend the final round of the National Jousting Match. To travel to this event in a timely manner, it is imperative that my carriage meet me immediately after the ceremony. Therefore, I will not miss your nuptials entirely. I am certain you will understand the importance of this invitation.

Your Father

Cinderella did *not* understand the importance of that invitation at such a time in her life. She was teary-eyed for three days and her father was nowhere to be seen.

If only her dear mother were at her side. She pictured her mother lying ill, stoically holding her pain within. Cinderella was only eight years old, but she was at her mother's bedside for two months, bringing her meals and keeping a damp rag on her forehead to lower the fever. During those months Cinderella would never know when her father would appear or vanish for days, never saying where he was going. Thinking back, Cinderella realized how her father made her feel almost invisible. When she spoke to him of any problems, he would merely nod and turn away. Her mother was her only confidante. She passed away a week before

Cinderella's ninth birthday. One of the few times her father held her hand was when her mother was lowered into her grave.

She pushed those old memories aside and decided she would enjoy every moment of her wedding. She told herself, "What was then, is over. Now I will be happy with Prince."

The wedding was even more lavish and romantic than the ball where Cinderella and Prince met. The music featured 18 trumpets, 23 violins, five oboes, and a harpsichord. Delicacies included squash soup, pheasant, beef Wellington and apple and cherry pies. A twelve-layer wedding cake was baked to symbolize the midnight hour at which Cinderella ran from the ball. Topping the cake was a glass slipper made of marzipan. Thousands of pink and yellow roses adorned the hall. There was dancing and merriment for the six hundred and thirteen guests.

After the ceremony, Judge Goodfellow delivered a warmhearted toast to the couple. He spoke of Cinderella meeting Prince's needs, and how "Prince, in his quiet, methodical manner" would provide for Cinderella. He told how "Cinderella is as kind and exuberant as she is beautiful." Many smiled when he suggested that Cinderella would keep both glass slippers on her feet today. The judge urged the couple to produce progeny to further the leadership of the kingdom. Laughter resonated throughout the hall when he said, "I know the King and Queen wish that you should not tarry even a single eve!"

Cinderella, Prince, and the King and Queen sat at the King's head table as the meal was served. From the corner of her eye Cinderella saw her father depart from a side door for the jousting tournament. She wished he had come over to express his joy and bid her adieu. Her stepmother and stepsisters were not seated at the King's table and Cinderella noticed her stepmother pouting. Later, as stepmother and stepsisters passed through the receiving line, Grouchina, the elder sister, whispered, " 'Tis so far away that we sit. The music barely reaches us. 'Tis a shame you treat your family thus!" Her stepmother also muttered a few words.

Cinderella kissed each on the cheek and said, "So sorry," forcing a smile. Prince pursed his lips and turned away quickly, greeting the next guests. Her stepmother grumbled her way back to her assigned table.

That afternoon, rice was thrown over the newlyweds as they entered their carriage. The King and Queen waved them off as six white horses sped the newlyweds down the hill from the palace. Cinderella's stepmother and stepsisters had edged themselves directly behind the King and Queen, waving as though *they* were the title holders of the castle. In the safety of the carriage, Cinderella sighed while Prince gently kissed her lips. The horses galloped until the wedding guests faded into dots and Cinderella squeezed Prince's hand.

II
The Honeymoon

THE HONEYMOON at the King's ocean side villa was both miraculous and enchanting to Cinderella. Soon after the coach delivered them, she grabbed Prince's hand and pulled him to the veranda, which overlooked the rocky beach and rolling ocean. Prince smiled, recognizing for the first time the full beauty of the landscape which he had taken for granted throughout his childhood.

Prince faced Cinderella and gently held her hands. "Dearest, are not the waves magnificent? Such a gorgeous day in May. I am the luckiest prince on earth!"

"And am I not fortunate to have you as my devoted husband? Isn't it wonderful that I have found you? I am certain we will live daily in this bliss. Just look around at your father's villa. What could be prettier? What could be more lovely than for us to stay here for a fortnight!"

Prince, in his quiet way, smiled, then picked up a stone and threw it over the hillside. They watched as it bounced off the boulders below and splashed into the turbulent waters.

Cinderella thought of how, so recently, she was at the mercy of her stepmother and how life had a way of rewarding those who were most in distress.

From the moment they arrived, the servants fulfilled their every wish. The King's personal chef prepared their meals. They dined in a room of mirrors with gilded frames. After dinner, the kingdom's finest musicians played their oboes, violins, and a harp. Later that evening, the court jester entertained with both fascinating and comical tales.

In the morn, Cinderella and Prince took breakfast on the veranda. Side by side, as the sun reflected on the ocean, they looked out upon their future together. All they saw was a halo of happiness.

At first, Cinderella was uncomfortable with physical intimacy. Her mother had never explained such activities and she had only heard whispers of it as she matured. But after a few nights, she felt the ecstasy of their lovemaking. From Prince's loving words, she knew his expectations were also far exceeded.

They basked in the joy that couples in love experience when their love is tender and unconditional, when their trust is full, and when their life partner is also their best friend.

On the last honeymoon eve, just before they snuffed the candles, Cinderella looked into Prince's eyes and said, "As I was cleaning the ashes from the fireplace a month afore, I never dreamed of such a time! I prayed on my mother's grave that I would win one such as you, and my prayers have been answered!"

Prince beamed. He stroked Cinderella's glowing cheeks and eagerly kissed her lips. They slept with arms entwined.

III

Palace Life

CINDERELLA was eager to return from their honeymoon and live in Prince's palace. Prince had the palace constructed two years earlier, knowing he would find a suitable bride to share his life. Returning from their honeymoon, Cinderella had difficulty imagining what her life would be like without her stepmother and stepsisters continually criticizing her.

That first day in the palace with only Prince and the servants was astonishing. She hopped around like a young girl about to open her birthday presents. Prince's face glowed as he saw Cinderella running through the chambers, admiring the elaborate furnishings and inspecting the paintings and gilded mirrors that decorated the walls. Occasionally, she would stare at the draperies or upholstery and suggest a fabric or color change. Prince would agree, even though he had made the original selections. Cinderella was ecstatic when she saw the magnificent gardens and she ran and twirled around the elliptical goldfish pond which faced their bed-room window.

The following day the Queen's courier delivered a note inviting Prince and Cinderella to dine with the King and Queen that very evening. Cinderella was befuddled, not knowing what to wear and fearing that she had not yet learned sufficient etiquette to attend such an important din-ner. She expressed her concerns to Prince who shrugged and said to "just act normally" and his parents would be "pleased as punch."

Cinderella examined her wardrobe, which her stepsisters and the tailor designed and, after much deliberation, chose a lace dress to be worn with a single strand of pearls. A few hours later she was prepared and stepped tentatively into the carriage for their trip to the King's palace, hoping she would find a way to assure herself that her evening performance would pass the princess-daughter-in-law assessment. As four black stallions carried them along a muddy road, Cinderella glanced down at her dress, then smiled at Prince, wishing he would say that she was dressed appropriately and looked lovely, but he only commented on the height of the wheat fields and breed of cattle the carriage was passing.

When the butler announced their arrival, Cinderella peered into the grand foyer, impatient to discover how the Queen was attired. Cinderella's mouth turned dry as they waited and Prince chatted with the butler. She thought she saw the butler wink at Prince after inquiring about their honeymoon.

The Queen was attired in a plain peasant blouse and country skirt, but admired Cinderella's more elaborate dress and necklace. As they sat at the dinner table, white wines and pâtés were served while Prince described how the exquisite weather increased the beauty of the honeymoon villa and ocean setting, which brought smiles to the King and Queen.

The conversation continued to flow and Cinderella's posture relaxed, allowing her to use a flourish of words to banter with the King and Queen. She told them how Prince's palace was more than she could have ever hoped for. She said how much she loved the gardens, the fish pond and the horse stables. The evening was pleasant and uneventful until bread and butter was served. Cinderella was still commenting on the palace, noting "we are planning a few modifications," when, without thought, she grabbed a knife to butter her bread as the others had already done. The Queen quickly pursed her lips, then bit her bottom lip while focusing on Cinderella's right hand. A moment later she turned to meet Prince's eyes and then, once again focused on Cinderella's hand.

Holding the knife in mid-air, Cinderella noticed she was not using the short, blunt-edged knife which the others had used, but one that had lain closer to the plate which had a long, sharp blade. She dropped the knife as if it were burning her fingers and it struck her plate with such a loud clunk that the others looked to see if the plate had cracked. Slowly she took hold of the shorter, blunt etched knife and buttered her bread while avoiding the Queen's eyes.

"And tell us, Cinderella, how was it that you began to live with your stepmother?" the Queen asked.

Cinderella, carefully and in a subdued, even pitch, recited a brief history of her mother's death and her father's remarriage. She paused, then offered, "And though my stepmother and stepsisters meant well toward me, we have had some differences in our way of thinking. Perhaps they believed father and I were not of equal stature." As the room became silent, she glanced at the Queen's face which had turned somber. Under the table Cinderella's fingernail pushed through her dress into her thigh until she felt a twinge of pain.

As the four of them sat quietly, barely moving, they could hear the rattling of dishes in the kitchen. Finally, Prince turned toward the King and inquired as to the size of the cattle herds in nearby kingdoms. The evening ended with a cursory handshake from the King and Queen before the butler showed Cinderella and Prince to their carriage.

They rode without speaking for awhile, Prince holding tight to Cinderella's arm and forcing a smile. Then he said, "A lovely evening. I believe they think highly of you."

Cinderella shook her head. "They think me a fool. The Queen was mortified when I used the incorrect knife and she believes you married below your stature. Oh, Prince, how will I ever gain her respect?"

"Nonsense, they already respect you for your kindness and beauty."

"I wish it were true. I think your mother wanted you to marry a real princess."

"No, no she is…she was… well, you are right." Prince swallowed hard and gathered his thoughts. "Over the years Mum had invited princesses from other kingdoms to dine, but she found that none were equal to me. Though she often points out my inadequacies privately, whenever she met princesses whose hand I might take, she deemed them beneath my stature. Her opinions have always been quite confusing."

"You? She found you possessed inadequacies?" Cinderella was incredulous. "Why, if you are not adequate in all ways, who could be?"

"Well, she finds the King is much more intelligent, and though I have tried, I have never been able to dissuade her from these feelings. Unlike Mum, I believed some of the princesses were certainly of high enough stature, though none of them were to my liking until I met you. When I spoke with you at the ball, I wanted to talk and talk and talk until the end of time!"

Cinderella squeezed Prince's hand and without hesitation kissed him so lovingly and with such passion that the coachman dared not turn to see what was occurring.

IV

The First Awareness
A Loving Relationship Requires
Daily Appreciations

PRINCE felt that, as the mistress of the palace, Cinderella must manage the royal household. He decided to delegate palace management to the servants for several weeks after the honeymoon, while Cinderella became accustomed to palace life. Though she found her new life exciting, it was so contrary to her upbringing that she felt quite awkward.

Within one month after their nuptials, Prince had taught Cinderella how to complete each palace task. She knew his heart was kind, but his instructional voice stirred up memories of her stepmother inspecting her work while she scrubbed the floors.

On the day when she was fully charged with palace management, Prince repeated countless times that she "must be fair, but firm with the servants." He told her, "They must understand that you, Cinderella, are the mistress of this house and that you are in full control. They must know that if their work is unsatisfactory, they will be discharged."

After Prince departed for work that day, Cinderella was alone with the servants. There were so many chambers in the palace that she hadn't even remembered them all. She sat near the fireplace, befuddled. *Be fair, but firm with them,* swirled in her head.

Soon, the head chambermaid approached to inquire if the master chamber should be cleaned. Cinderella simply nodded and said, "Yes, please." Then realizing she had not sounded very firm, she added loudly, "And make sure it is *thoroughly cleaned from top to bottom!*"

The chambermaid was clearly taken aback. "Yes, Madam, of course," she said meekly and walked away. Cinderella continued to sit near the fireplace, feeling in her heart that she was not going to be good at directing others, for she knew only how to perform the work herself.

When Prince returned from work, all the tasks were completed. Cinderella described how she had supervised each one. All he said was "yes," and proceeded to talk about his day.

Cinderella received no praise from Prince during the following months. Day after day, from morn to evening, she worked diligently to manage the palace, and day after day she waited to hear a simple "good" or "thank you" or "very fine." She heard nothing.

She had made sure the bread was baked, vegetables were prepared, the meat was cured, chambers were cleaned, the garden was cared for, and palace walls were repaired. Prince would return from work and merely say "yes" when she told him of her efforts. It reminded her of never receiving a single compliment from her father or stepmother. She told herself that Prince was not mean, just busy. But *Oh!*, she wished, if only he would say *thank you* or *fine work* even once!

He acted as though he really didn't care. When she told him of her day, he interrupted and spoke only about his. Her stomach churned as though it were making butter. "I guess his work managing the kingdom *is* much more important than my work," she thought.

Three months after the honeymoon, she sat in the parlour and tears flowed, "Oh, what unhappiness I have here! I thought marrying Prince would fill me with joy. Now I find my duties are no better than living with my stepmother. He doesn't care about me at all!" She lay on the settee, resting her head on a satin pillow. She dreamt of a time when her mother was holding her to her bosom.

A while later, Cinderella awakened to a rustling sound. She looked up and saw Fairy Godmother floating down toward her. She was a small delicate lady, dressed in a plain white pinafore of cotton batiste, with a pastel bodice of dotted Swiss. She held the same silver wand that she used to prepare Cinderella for the ball. Her soft white hair was adorned with a fine silver ribbon.

Fairy Godmother's powerful presence disguised her short stature. Her large grey-green eyes invited Cinderella in, and it pleased Cinderella that Fairy Godmother had been able to discern that she was unhappy and had come to her assistance.

"My child, what in heaven's name is wrong?"

"Oh, Fairy Godmother, my life is no happier than before. Prince doesn't appreciate me. He offers me no praise for my work, nor for anything I do."

"So he does not praise you as you praise him?"

This question confused Cinderella because she had not thought she was required to praise Prince since he was, well, a prince.

"A prince needs praise?" she finally asked.

"He's a prince, but also a man. And men need much praise, though they often act as if 'tis not important, for hidden inside the mind of all men are the feelings of the little boy from which they grew. Each woman also carries her little girl within her."

"But, surely a lady shan't offer compliments first. 'Tis the duty of a gentleman to first offer respect and admiration to his lady!"

Fairy Godmother tilted her head in a curious manner before saying:

Which comes first, the chicken or the egg?
A riddle, a puzzle, pray tell me, I beg.

"Wha—what?" said Cinderella, quite puzzled herself, trying to decipher the words.

With a slight smile, Fairy Godmother added:

> *Where, oh where, doth the praise begin,*
> *Someone must start, or no one will win!*

"Oh…. Oh, I see," Cinderella said, realizing that in every activity someone must go first.

Just before she floated out of the room, Fairy Godmother said:

> *As water and sunshine make flowers bloom,*
> *Praise is required of the bride and the groom;*
> *Praise can be offered in three different flavours:*
> *His appearance, character, or his behaviours.*

Cinderella was much too engaged in following this rhyme to worry about how Fairy Godmother appeared or disappeared from the parlour, and it was a few minutes before she realized she was alone.

"Aha!" she thought. "Three different flavours like candy or cakes. So Prince needs compliments, too. He seems so self-assured that I never would have thought it." She glanced outside at the garden, radiant with daisies in the noonday sun.

When Prince's carriage rolled up to the palace in late afternoon, she greeted him outside near the rose bushes, rather than waiting for him to enter.

"Your hair has been shorn in an appealing manner. You

are looking quite handsome today!" Cinderella said, beaming at him.

Prince raised his chin, smiled so his teeth shone bright, then took her hand and stroked it. He gently kissed the back of each finger. It thrilled her that he was so touched by her loving words.

While dining that eve, Cinderella told Prince that she knew how hard he worked, regularly attending the business of the kingdom on all days except when they worshipped. Prince immediately spoke proudly of his efforts to help the people of the kingdom with new roads and additional knights to protect the village homes. He was obviously pleased that Cinderella had praised his hardworking "character" and called for the court jester to entertain them that evening.

Later, Cinderella said to Prince, "I thank thee so much for selecting such a comical court jester this night. I felt more cared for tonight than at any time since our honeymoon." The love they made that night continued well into morn.

While Prince was at work, Cinderella unrolled a parchment, opened her inkwell, and penned:

Praise Often

Praise can be offered
In three different flavours:
Appearance, character,
Or one's good behaviours.

Appearance: His engaging smile, his dashing hair, his comely clothes, his masculine unclothed body.

Behaviour: How he plans outings with me, what he does for others, how he listens to me, how he makes love with me.

Character: His sense of humour, his intelligence, his ability to work hard, his athletic strength in jousting, his knowledge of music.

She hid the parchment in her bureau beneath her personal belongings.

What Cinderella Learned About Appreciations

In the months that followed, Cinderella sought and found ways to praise Prince. As she searched, she realized he pleased her in so many ways. At first it was awkward expressing her appreciation, but Fairy Godmother had emphasized its importance, so Cinderella made a great effort to praise him every day in some way.

Cinderella heard from others about Prince's work in the kingdom, and she told him how wonderful it was that he was aiding both the wealthy and the poor. Prince, buoyed by her enthusiasm, became more talkative. Gradually, he began to speak of his appreciation for her skills in maintaining the palace. He also commented on how the meals she planned were more and more sumptuous and how her new tulip garden near the pond made him glow. As she felt appreciated, Cinderella's earlier frustrations faded and she became more comfortable in her marriage. Her new life began to blossom.

Of course conflicts still arose between them, but by giving and receiving praise, the couple developed a mutual trust and respect that enabled them to discuss their differences with civil tongues. She found they were using the word "we" more frequently when they expressed their wishes and dreams.

V

The Second Awareness
A Loving Relationship Requires Accepting Each Other's Perspective and Feelings

HE MOUSE incident occurred on Friday, February 13th. Prince remembered it well; it happened the day before Valentine's Day. As everyone knew, Valentine's Day was the day birds began to mate, so the custom was for men to write amorous letters to their lovers. But this year a small mouse delayed Prince's letter to Cinderella.

Until this day Prince knew what to expect after work: Cinderella would greet him in the vestibule; they would embrace and take a cup of tea in the parlour. Then he would tell her how he managed to deal with the problems in the kingdom. Frequently, he would brag of outmaneuvering the King by presenting impressive proposals. She never failed to speak highly of his work and would even giggle as he described his accomplishments in great detail.

Prince discovered their love was rekindled after Cinderella began to praise him. It became natural for him in turn to recognize her fine work in managing the castle, admire her beauty, and compliment her sparkling conversation when they visited friends.

Once when she didn't know he had entered the master chamber, he heard her singing:

As water and sunshine make flowers bloom,
Praise is required of the bride and the groom.

However, on this Friday, the butler appeared at the door and simply announced that Cinderella was in her boudoir. As Prince walked through the main hall, he peered into the dining room. The table was not set for dinner, and the chairs were in disarray and grouped near the corner of the room.

He hurried up the stairs to find Cinderella perched on a settee with her legs avoiding the floor. Her face was flushed and she was teary-eyed.

"Oh, Prince! You can't imagine how awful this day has been! I saw a *mouse* scurry across the ballroom floor!"

Prince screwed up his face. "So what doth that mean?"

"*So what doth that mean?* You cannot understand that there was a large mouse, maybe a rat, that almost bit my leg and he's running wild in our home?"

"Have you completed all the household chores today?" was all Prince could think of asking.

"Don't you — can't you understand? How can I talk to the servants when a huge, vicious rat runs loose here?"

Prince did not understand her peculiar thoughts. He knew a mouse was no more a danger than a pigeon! It makes a noise and it scurries away.

Earlier, on his carriage ride home, Prince had thought how he would announce to Cinderella his great news: He had been named Captain of the kingdom's jousting team and he would be traveling to Joustershire Kingdom in a fortnight for the regional match. Instead, he found himself being bothered by a silly little mouse!

Burdened with Cinderella's outlandish outburst, he knew he must maintain his princely control or she might believe she could get away with this nonsense. After all, the man, not the lady, is in charge of the palace! If she were allowed to lead, she might spend years having tea parties with her lady friends and never tend to the household. Maybe when their children were birthed, she would not care for them properly, either!

A childhood memory flashed before him. His father was entertaining a visiting king and Prince's mother had failed in her duties. He heard his father's words: "My lady did not supervise the cooks today and allowed them to overcook the beef! The beef tasted as the tongue of my boot! Ah, yea, as the tongue of my left boot!" The Queen's eyes had filled with tears while his father leaned toward her with his lips held tight and hands on his hips.

Prince decided he must nip Cinderella's behavior in the bud.

"You are the mistress of this house! Being fearful of a small mouse will not serve you well. Are you not responsible for making sure the cook bakes the bread and the chambermaids clean the chambers? Are you not *fully* responsible for assuring that the gardener tends the garden and the repairmen maintain the palace walls?" Prince's face reddened as his eyes focused squarely on Cinderella's face.

Tears streamed down Cinderella's cheeks. She turned away from Prince, holding her shawl tightly between her fingers, dabbing at her tears. She tried to talk. At first no sounds arose. Then she sputtered, "But there was this – this, dangerous ra- rat eating its way through the pal—, through the palace, waiting to pounce on me! He must have been bigger than a cat! How could I possibly take care of chores on such a d- da- day!"

Prince's voice deepened as he explained the facts: "There are mice in all palaces. Mice and rats are much more afraid of you than you are of them. They scurry away, as I'm sure this one did. Yes, they sometimes chew a chair, but they are not dangerous. If you are afraid of a little rodent, how will you ever maintain the palace?"

Cinderella shivered. She rose and began to run. She ran down the hall holding her dress close so it wouldn't brush the marble floor. She ran faster than she had run when she was escaping the ball after the clock struck twelve. Behind her, she heard Prince hollering. He sounded much like her stepmother screaming for her to polish the silver.

"And," Prince yelled, "Perhaps I should have chosen a lady of a suitable rank who has been trained to manage such a large palace. Perhaps I should have discovered earlier that you have the fears of a little girl!"

That evening, Cinderella and Prince took separate meals. Before the candles were snuffed for the night, Cinderella vacated the master chamber and slept alone in a guest chamber. She dreamt she was back in her mother's arms being cradled.

When she awoke, she looked through her bedroom window and saw the sun's rays bouncing off the fish pond which lay beyond the rear garden. Prince's carriage had left for his office in the King's castle.

In his office chamber, Prince sat alone. He tried to swallow his lunch of kidney pie and Yorkshire pudding. "She is fearful of a little mouse," he thought. "The palace is full of mice and they have never harmed a soul. If she spends all day fearful of a mouse, how will she organize the household of cooks, maids and butlers? Maybe I was too hasty in selecting a bride. Maybe we aren't meant for each other!"

He rose from his work table and paced the room once, twice, maybe a dozen times. His mind was spinning ways to convince Cinderella that there was no need to be frightened of a mouse. How absurd! Never in a hundred years would a mouse hurt her. Prince walked the floor a few more times, absentmindedly counting the large granite slabs. He peeked through the curtains and saw the King's stallions being groomed. I have all this and a bride who does not obey me. What have I done? I was much too hasty! After all, I only saw her one evening before our marriage and she left prematurely.

He remembered their honeymoon and their lovemaking. He thought of how Cinderella admired him when he told her of the new carriage roads he was constructing. In his mind's eye, he could hear her cheering him on when she attended his jousting match. *I know what I'll do! I will get the Royal Recorder to list the number of times when there have been mice hurting anyone in the kingdom during the last twenty years. I'll present the facts to Cinderella and she will realize how foolish she is. Then we can make amends and we will revisit our joyful times.*

He was weary from a fitful night's sleep. He placed his head on his work table next to his half-eaten Yorkshire pudding. A while later, he awoke to find a short, slight man with a long, grey beard seated on the chair across from him. The man wore short black leather pants with a golden chain for a belt. Sewn across the front of his ruffled white shirt were three red triangular buttons, with no apparent purpose. A bright blue kerchief adorned his neck. He wore leather boots that curled up at the toe almost like a snail's shell. Prince could not recall ever seeing such fashions.

"May I be of assistance?" Prince asked.

"Not at all, but as your Caring Godfather, I presume I can be of assistance to you with Mistress Cinderella."

"Oh!" was all Prince heard himself say.

Prince was eager for any advice, especially from Caring Godfather. He had never met the man, but Prince's grandfather had told him that Caring Godfather was of enormous aid whenever he had difficulty understanding Prince's grandmother.

Prince nodded. "Yes, I certainly do need help convincing my wife that a mouse can do no harm."

"Not a good idea. Not a fine idea at all," Caring Godfather said, shaking his head as if he were trying to rid a fly from his fine, white hair. "The solution is much simpler than you think."

"If it please you, Caring Godfather, it would delight me enormously to resolve this issue and again reach joyful times with Cinderella. I want a final end to any dissension we might ever have."

"Oh, it will never be a final end. With love conflicts, nothing is ever final!" The old man's gentle smile blanketed Prince with trust. "No, I'm afraid with marriage, the end appears and reappears as if it were a ring rolling down a curvy road. But follow this simple truth, which will stead you with your wife:

Remember the physician Hippocrates, who wrote of our emotions,
From the brain arise our pleasures, our sorrows and painful potions;

*That Greek has said our sleepless nights are
structured in our brain,
We believe those "facts" the cause, of this we must
abstain;
'Tis a truth of life, emotions must be accepted,
She will surely break your heart whene'er she feels
rejected;
You needn't agree, or think as she, to have a loving
marriage,
Facts and figures have no part, feelings shan't be
disparaged!*

Prince turned toward the window to place Caring Godfather's words on the pane. He tried to fit them into the mouse puzzle. "Facts, figures have no part....emotions must be accepted....?"

When he glanced back, the old man was no longer there.

Prince felt he must try on Caring Godfather's ideas, even if they were not tailored to his own thinking. After all, he had already explained the facts about mice to Cinderella, to no avail. He hurried into the King's library and read sections of the ancient book, *The Sacred Disease*, by Hippocrates. Yes, Caring Godfather was correct. Prince read that the same brain that helps solve analytical problems uses different parts to carry joy, laughter, pain, worry and, Hippocrates stated: "whether by night or by day, brings us sleeplessness." He realized it would be more fruitful to accept Cinderella's emotions, whatever they may be, instead of trying to replace hers with his. How logical! How easy!

When he returned to his castle, Cinderella was in the wine cellar with Beetrice, the head cook. They were planning a special recipe, coq au vin. Cinderella stared up the steps as Prince approached.

"I'm sorry," he began, looking down into the wine cellar.

"What?" she said in disbelief, seeing his weary eyes and realizing that he, too, must have had very little sleep.

"I'm sorry I didn't let you explain all that happened. I'd like to hear about the mouse."

"'Twas nothing." She shrugged. "We need not speak of it."

Seeing her taut jaw, Prince knew otherwise.

"Pray tell? Pray tell what you saw and how it was for you?" He walked her into the parlour.

As they sat with a pot of tea, Prince took her hand between the two of his and focused on her face.

There she told him of her fright, how her knees trembled and how she was sure the "small mouse" would bite her fingers. She told him that, since Fairy Godmother had changed mice into horses, somehow this mouse might acquire the characteristics of a vicious dog or even a lion!

She spoke of how she was ashamed that she had not managed the household properly yesterday and how she feared he would reprimand her again. Prince saw her face calming and a greater beauty gracing her cheeks. He asked her to tell him even more, trying with all his faculties to think and feel what it would be like if he were Cinderella and he had been terribly frightened by a mouse that might become a lion.

That evening, Prince declared, so loudly that his voice echoed throughout the palace, that the feast of coq au vin was tastier than any meal he had ever consumed. And later that evening, with their arms entwined, Prince knew he had chosen his bride well.

The next day, after he arrived for work, he penned on parchment:

True Love Requires Accepting Each Other's Feelings and Perspectives

♦ *I needn't feel as you*
♦ *I merely need to understand and accept your feelings and listen fully*

Prince placed the parchment in his **IMPORTANT PARCHMENTS** cabinet. How wise it was to just listen and understand her viewpoint, and then the two could feel much calmer. He realized that offering facts and analyses were quite useful in talking to the King about managing the kingdom. However, facts and analyses would hit him as a boomerang if he tried to do the same when speaking with Cinderella about her feelings.

What Prince Learned from a Little Mouse

In the weeks that followed, Prince began to understand how some of his words stirred Cinderella's emotions. At times he thought he was merely providing facts to help her understand a situation, but she perceived the information quite differently and she felt dishonoured.

In the palace library he studied the writings of the ancient Greeks, Plato and Aristotle. Relevant to harmony in marriage, the philosophers alluded to two different areas of the brain: One area analyzes facts and the other area expresses emotions. Often a person is so intent on presenting what he believes to be the facts that he does not realize he is ignoring his partner's feelings. To maintain harmony, each person needs to listen and accept the other's emotions.

Emotions develop from one's childhood experiences and are so solidly anchored that each partner will fight vigorously if one tells the other how they should feel. Prince thought he was just being factual when discussing Cinderella's fear of a mouse, but in doing so he had stirred Cinderella's emotions.

Prince now realized he was taught by his parents to hide his emotions since they thought exhibiting feelings was a sign of weakness. However, Cinderella took Prince to be cold and insincere if he did not openly express all his emotions.

The mouse incident taught Prince that true love could only be realized and maintained if Cinderella and he expressed and *accepted* each other's emotions, even when their beliefs were contrary. Yes, Prince learned a great deal from Plato, Aristotle, and from a little mouse.

VI

The Third Awareness
A Loving Relationship Requires Supporting Each Other When Relatives Interfere

NE DAY a messenger delivered the following note:

Dearest Sister Cinderella,

I thank thee for supporting thy family after thy nuptials. Mother and sister also express gratitude. (Of course, if circumstances were reversed, we would have done so precisely.) However, the Duke and I cannot contend with our present situation brought on by Prince. The land Prince has bestowed upon us is much too small for the house we wish to construct and would not offer an attractive view. How could we possibly raise a family on such a small estate? All that is required is for Prince to provide us with the Weatherspoons' parcel one mile to the east, which

overlooks the valley. I'm sure Prince can find
another suitable parcel for the Weatherspoons.
Mr. Weatherspoon, as everyone knows, is merely a
tinsmith.

I expect this will be cared for in a timely fashion.

> *Your loving sister,*
> *Grouchina*

Cinderella read the note numerous times. She heard her mother's voice saying "…and families must bond together…and families must bond together…"

What should she tell Prince? He believed he had been so gracious in providing his stepsisters-in-law any land at all. "Should not each duke purchase the land for himself?" he had asked. Cinderella had persuaded him that the kingdom contained sufficient square miles for all, and that sisters must support each other. In the end, an adequate parcel was conveyed to each duke whom Cinderella's stepsisters had married.

After dinner that evening, Cinderella told Prince she had a wish. Because of the harmony in the palace, Prince was ready to listen. But then he heard a request he thought quite unreasonable.

"What!" he said, loud enough to be heard in the servants' quarters. "They ask for even more? They made me a fool to have offered *any* parcel, considering the treatment they bestowed on you!"

He left the table and dashed out the rear to the stables. Cinderella saw him saddle his favourite mare and gallop westward.

For days, they did not speak of the issue, yet each felt the chill. They were cordial and spoke of the weather and the cattle being raised in a nearby kingdom. No further words were exchanged about Grouchina's request. For ten days, which felt much longer to Cinderella, she bedded earlier than Prince and they did not entwine.

Then, the same messenger arrived with a second note:

Dearest Sister Cinderella,

I have heard no word from thee for almost a fortnight. I am a patient woman, but the situation requires a transfer of the Weatherspoons' parcel to us tout-de-suite. I fear the Weatherspoons will commence construction of their home and 'twould be a pity to require destruction of a new frame.

Your loving sister,
Grouchina

Cinderella again heard her mother's voice. "Those who have, should support those in need. Support your family, as I have supported you, for that is the essence of kindness." As she reread Grouchina's note, her head spun and her knees felt weak. She clutched the note and lay down on the settee. "When should I approach Prince?" she wondered. "I have no choice; I must support my sister. As she has said, she would have done the same."

She brushed wisps of hair from her face and when she glanced up, Fairy Godmother was floating down, barely touching the floor with her toes. Her wand glistened from the sun streaming through the window. She looked upon Cinderella.

"My! My! I find thee in torment today."

"Oh, Fairy Godmother, 'tis awful that I must speak to Prince about Grouchina's quandary."

"Grouchina has a quandary? Strange that *you* have the distress."

"Well, as a good sister, I have no choice but to help her obtain a suitable parcel for her house."

"Hmmm," was all Fairy Godmother would say.

"You see, she has too small a parcel with no quality view of the valley."

"Hmmm," Fairy Godmother repeated.

"So when should I explain to Prince what is needed?"

"Haven't you already done so?"

"Well, he became angry and we spoke no more."

"So, it is his responsibility to parcel out land?"

"Oh, yes. He is the master of such decisions."

"Well, Cinderella, receive advice thus:"

> *Conventions of family relationship require,*
> *Grouchina speak with thy powerful squire;*

Tête-à-tête relationships always must decide,
Behind a third party, Grouchina cannot hide;

When three different people seek a solution,
The triangle causes extreme convolution.

Cinderella felt a sudden relief, as if seeing Fairy Godmother float out of the chamber carried the stress from her body. Her head was calm. She no longer felt too warm.

So Grouchina must speak directly with Prince, and he must decide.

Without hesitating she drew her goose quill, dabbed it into the inkwell and penned:

My Dear Sister Grouchina,

I received your thoughtful note this morn. I fully understand your desires concerning a new property. However, as you know, it is not my, but Prince's responsibility to make such land decisions in the kingdom. Therefore, it is incumbent upon you to put your request to him directly. I am sure an appropriate decision can be reached.

Your loving sister,
Cinderella

She placed her wax seal firmly on the folded note and sent her messenger on the swiftest palace stallion to deliver it. Then she requested that her bath be drawn and luxuriated in an abundance of suds. After bathing, she felt radiant in her dressing gown and inscribed on a parchment the following:

Triangles Beget Conflict

A peaceful, loving relationship requires,
That intervention by relatives not
*   transpire;*
When three different people seek a
*   solution,*
The triangle causes extreme convolution;
When they make unfair requests,
Kin must be told where judgment rests.

Cinderella placed the parchment in her bureau beneath her personal belongings and fastened the lock.

Over time, Cinderella and Prince learned that family triangles arise more often than weeds in the rose garden.

What Cinderella Learned About Dealing with Relatives

Families can foster great happiness for couples or cause major harm. It is wonderful to have parents, siblings, and relatives join in celebrations and feel the closeness of those who care. Sometimes it is useful to consult relatives when one has a special problem that only a relative can help solve. However, too much control from the outside will split a couple's loyalty.

Cinderella and Prince learned that their primary loyalty must be for each other even when they didn't see eye to eye. Their disputes always grew worse when relatives intervened. They learned that while their relatives often tried to help, this intrusion resulted in greater stress on their marriage.

Cinderella was very clear with her stepsister. Grouchina must contact Prince directly with her concerns about where to construct her house. Prince, in similar form, would tell his mother that he did not want to hear her complaints about Cinderella. He made it clear that the Queen should speak directly to his wife with such concerns, since he knew that "a third wheel will steer a wagon off the proper path."

VII

The Fourth Awareness
A Loving Relationship Requires Togetherness

OUSTING consumed much of Prince's spare time. Cinderella would bring her embroidery and pretend to watch the entire match, but in fact she was frightened by the brutal clashes of the men in armour. Often Prince's arm or leg would be dripping blood when he dismounted his steed. Though she couldn't bear to see him suffer, she recognized his love of the sport, so she would cheer him on during the match.

When they were first wed, jousting practice was held on Thursday afternoons. Prince would leave work early, practice, and return for dinner afore sunset. However, over time, he added Tuesday to his practice and then Wednesday. Finally, before a regional meet he would practice for four solid weeks after work and then they would dine quite late.

With these schedule changes, Cinderella busied herself

with embroidery or spent the time planning the week's palace repairs. She was quite lonely waiting for him. When he did return, it seemed to take hours until he bathed and was set to dine. The lonely feeling reminded her of how her father would, without a word, disappear on a voyage and then reappear, only to occupy himself with his personal matters.

Cinderella was so deprived of a loving connection that she could no longer bear it. To ease her loneliness, she took to visiting the Duchess of Gossipwich in late afternoons. The Duchess was also alone since the Duke of Gossipwich had boarded ship for a two-year voyage to explore a foreign land. Cinderella and the Duchess would speak of their mutual hardships, and how unfair it was to be deserted. Each expressed deep empathy toward the other.

In early evening, the Duchess would serve hors-d'œuvres to stem Cinderella's appetite until Prince returned for a late dinner. Over the weeks, Cinderella extended her visits with the Duchess through the evening meal. When she returned home late to greet Prince, he was exhausted so he had little desire to converse with her. During this time, his ardor fell, leading her to even greater frustration.

One Tuesday morn, Cinderella sat in her boudoir thinking, "If I tell Prince his excessive passion for jousting leads to my gloom, he may limit his practice but be resentful. If he reduces his practice, loses his regional matches and consequently cannot compete in the national competition, he would never forgive me, nor would I forgive myself. And yet, if he continues to be away, our true love will fade."

Though Cinderella's boudoir was on the second floor of the palace, somehow Fairy Godmother always found a way of quietly entering. Fairy Godmother had rarely seen such a cheerless countenance, and she told Cinderella so.

"Well, the condition is not possible to reconcile," Cinderella told Fairy Godmother. "Need I be a most dreadful wife and complain to Prince, or do I say naught and allow our love to suffer an unfortunate demise? 'Tis a quandary without a solution...." Cinderella's words trailed off and were replaced by sobs so loud that the windowpanes began to vibrate.

"Oh dear, oh dear, oh dear, Cinderella," Fairy Godmother said to calm her and waited a long time for her to quiet down.

"You see," Cinderella sniffled, "If I discourage Prince from jousting, he will despise me. Yet, if he continues his extensive sport, it will no longer be possible to converse and bond with him. If only he would not have taken up jousting! Perhaps it would have been better of me if I never had met him at the ball." Cinderella's sobbing resumed.

Fairy Godmother waited patiently and finally quieted Cinderella by saying, "What if there were a way to untie this knot? What if both Prince and thee could be joyful together?"

Cinderella bit her lip and adjusted her shoulders. She

looked up at Fairy Godmother who, despite her short stature, always seemed to be floating above Cinderella.

"A way to make us joyful once again? 'Tis possible?"

"Cinderella, you and Prince have learned to be aware of each other's needs. The kindness in your heart will stay you again."

Fairy Godmother's eye and wand both twinkled as she said:

> *When one spouse is consumed with interests,*
> *leaving the other behind,*
> *The result is that both will suffer with loneliness,*
> *you'll find;*
>
> *Talk to him and let him know precisely how you*
> *feel,*
> *His love for thee is much greater than any*
> *jousting zeal;*
>
> *If one spends too much time away, the other can't*
> *pretend,*
> *Sadness envelops both of you, both hearts must*
> *later mend.*

After Fairy Godmother left, Cinderella sat bewildered. She had heard Fairy Godmother's words but still could not envision talking "precisely" to Prince. She knew how much he loved jousting. She remembered the excitement that rose in his throat as he told her of his new tactics to unseat his next opponent. In her heart, she knew Prince truly loved her and had expressed it over and over.

Cinderella waited for an evening when Prince appeared calm to approach him. She even wrote out what she would say and rewrote it many times to assure herself that the words would be fair, yet hit their mark.

On that day he had delighted her with an ornamental fish for the pond. It was more colorful than any other, with white and blue markings and a large fan-like tail.

As they sat facing the fish pond, it seemed to be the perfect time for her to raise her concerns.

"Dearest," she began. Prince, who had sat motionless, staring at the fish chasing one another under the lily pads, turned toward her. "If you please, I would like to discuss something bothersome to me."

"What, my dear?" he asked, and she knew he was quite open to her concerns.

"'Tis the extent of your time at jousting. I so admire thy love of the sport, for each should continue what brings happiness."

She waited, holding her chest, dreading that she would be struck by a burst of anger. None came, so she continued, "But I fear the length and breadth of thy sport now divides us. It causes me much distress and loneliness. Is there a way? Is there a means? What I mean is, can we stay our friendship and— "

"My dear," Prince interjected. "Of late, I certainly have sensed our closeness diminishing." Cinderella nodded an invitation for Prince to continue.

"The sport does energize me and even takes hold more than I believed. However, the grueling practice leaves me with insufficient energy for you, my truest love. Would it be agreeable for thee if I prepare for one solid week before the final championship and Thursdays alone for the weekly matches on all other weeks?"

"Certainly," Cinderella said without hesitation, so grateful for Prince's thoughtful compromise. Cinderella could not believe the speed of Prince's decision. She knew from the past that change was often difficult, and she so appreciated his willingness to adjust his schedule. She also knew that as they had become more aware of ways to be closer, their love had grown and change had become easier for both of them. After he spoke, she looked up and smiled at the heavens.

The next morn she wrote the following and stored it with her personal belongings:

Loneliness Ensues When One Partner Avoids the Other

Too much time spent apart,
Leads to frailties of the heart;
Love in marriage necessitates,
Time for joy to celebrate.

What Cinderella Learned About Togetherness

Cinderella felt lonely when Prince was excessively involved with his activities. However, she also knew that he became lonely when she ignored him. In either case, emotional closeness was lost and both suffered.

Cinderella's relationship with the Duchess of Gossipwich illustrated this point. As her friendship with the Duchess grew, the two exchanged many notes. One day Prince asked Cinderella why she often sent a messenger to the Duchess' home. Dumbfounded, she stammered and finally confessed that she was writing in detail to the Duchess of how she was able to express her feelings of loneliness to Prince.

"What!" Prince demanded, "You are discussing our private life with others?"

This disagreement had a silver lining. They discussed the many ways that other people or events might cause their relationship to deteriorate. Whenever either felt that their emotional bond was lessening, they talked about the issue and each listened fully, accepting the other's feelings.

Prince and Cinderella realized that sometimes, if one was not listening to the other's feelings, they would seek outside activities as an escape. They agreed that when either felt the other was spending excessive time away, it interfered with their closeness and a talk was needed to recapture their loving relationship.

VIII

The Fifth Awareness
A Loving Relationship Requires Physical Intimacy

PHYSICAL INTIMACY waned over time. Prince would approach Cinderella several times a week in the evenings, as had been his practice. However, her enthusiasm was tempered in recent months. At times, she would acquiesce, but her spirits were subdued. On other evenings, she expressed a weakness from the day's work and went to bed directly after dining.

He began to question his lovemaking skills, on which he had previously prided himself. Each time she refused, his ardor rose rather than fell. He would see young maidens in town and think that they would be only too happy to share his bed. But he didn't desire them; he only wished to rekindle Cinderella's flame.

He thought about their wonderful honeymoon romance and how they had continued their exciting lovemaking in the palace over many months. But now he only wished he could find *any* approach that she would accept. He was frustrated that his ability to understand and correct the problems of the kingdom far outweighed his ability to understand Cinderella's diminishing desire for physical intimacy.

Prince began maintaining records of the different ways he had approached Cinderella and her encouraging or discouraging responses. He was The Prince of his kingdom and should certainly be able to devise a solution to such a situation. While at work, his concerns with Cinderella were only aggravated by the mountain of documents that required his stamp. It was in this state that Caring Godfather found him.

Caring Godfather sat on the ottoman, stroking his gray beard, his gold belt chain glimmering from the sunlight pouring through the windows.

"It appears, dear Prince, that thy lady is causing thee much distress."

"Oh, Caring Godfather! Cinderella has lost her love for me!" Prince cried out.

"Lost her love for ye? Pray tell?"

"Well, she rarely wishes to bed in a married way, and when she does, it is only to satisfy my desires."

Caring Godfather motioned for him to continue.

"When at first we wed, it was as much she as I, who wished to share our bed. But now she says she is fatigued, yet I see that she carries on with vigor during the day and well into the eve."

Caring Godfather responded, "Thee may find that her ardor grows most intense when thou shows intense interest in her."

"But certainly I have! I brought her many bouquets, she loves the fish I select for the pond, and just last week I presented her with ruby earrings. What more can my lady wish?"

"Presents are well and good. They are certain to do no harm, but what a lady requires is not simply gifts. Cinderella wants you to convey your respect and your interest in her daily being. She wishes for you to know that she is important to you and to the kingdom!" The volume of Caring Godfather's voice increased to match that of the robins chattering with each other outside the window.

Caring Godfather stroked his gray beard, giving Prince the feeling that it was important to listen to the wise counsel that was about to be offered:

> *When a woman's ardor wanes,*
> *When you approach but she abstains;*
> *Look well behind this tender issue,*
> *You will find she doth truly miss you.*
>
> *Thy lady wishes from you all seasons,*
> *To see her value for many reasons;*
> *If you give harbour to this advice,*
> *Intimacy for both will be thrice as nice!*

Physically, women have special desires,
You must search for what she requires;
Think of hers, not just your spice,
And intimacy for both will be thrice as nice!

After Caring Godfather rose out the window and up through the chestnut tree, miraculously not stirring any branch, Prince strolled the grounds near the King's palace. He listened to the love songs of the robins and sparrows. His eyes admired the beauty of the bright yellow tulips and deep purple irises waving in a gentle breeze. "I know that Cinderella is important to me for many reasons. But how do I tell her? How do I show her? Perhaps I have been delinquent in conveying my love."

Prince was determined. He called for his carriage to return him to the palace. Upon arrival, he found Cinderella saying adieu to two duchesses from the village. He remembered that she was having them over for tea to plan a new Food House for the poor. She greeted Prince with a hug and inquired about his day.

"My desire," said Prince, "is to hear tell of your plan for the new Food House."

Cinderella glowed at his request, for Prince had never before asked about this work. In fact, other than praise for her work in the castle and his comments about her beauty, he seldom took notice of other parts of her life.

She spoke energetically of how she and the two duchesses were developing the Food House in the town square. She told him how citizens who could ill afford wheat or potatoes would have a ration of each. She described the coal stove that would warm them and even straw mats that would be available for those whose homes had burned.

As she spoke, she looked into Prince's eyes to determine if he truly wanted to listen. To her astonishment, he not only wished to listen but asked if the King could help finance the venture to put fewer demands on the duchesses' contribution.

"Cinderella, it is glorious that you care, not solely for our palace, but for the needs of others!"

That evening, in bed, Prince spoke gently to Cinderella, hoping to discover her intimate needs. He then offered what she desired. Yes, he realized, Caring Godfather was right. By admiring her values and tending to her personal desires, intimacy *was* thrice as nice!

Prince saw how wonderful it was that she cared, not only for him, but for those who were less fortunate. He now knew that his pure love for Cinderella was founded on her many virtues.

The next day he wrote the following and placed the parchment in his **IMPORTANT PARCHMENTS** cabinet:

Physical Intimacy

Physical intimacy requires acknowledging my lady's importance and tending to her intimate desires.

What Prince Learned About Physical Intimacy

Over the months, Prince found that Cinderella felt closest and most intimate with him when he acknowledged her importance. He truly admired all her values. She cared for the poor of the kingdom by establishing Food Houses. She efficiently managed the beautiful palace and gardens with remarkable ease. When they were with friends, her charm was evident to all. Their intimacy grew as he appreciated the wonderful person that was *Cinderella!* Also, Prince found that if lovemaking became routine, it lost spirit. He learned that physical intimacy meant much more than their time spent in the master chamber. Both he and Cinderella often experienced intimacy while dining, by their endearing glances, with loving caresses, and by their exchange of warm, suggestive thoughts.

In addition, Prince found new ways to be intimately adventurous and asked Cinderella what pleased or displeased her. She then asked the same of him. They realized that their impetuous, spontaneous desires created ecstasy; but more often, scheduling for a special place and a variety of exciting ways worked best to maintain physical closeness.

They recreated their honeymoon over and over in different ways and different places. Yes, Prince found that joyous lovemaking, too, took planning and creativity, but *Oh! It was thrice as nice!*

IX

The Sixth Awareness
A Loving Relationship Requires Accepting Each Other's Different Values

BEING a prince means you are wealthy and you deserve privileges. As soon as he could speak, the King and Queen taught Prince this truism. He also knew there was only one way for the citizens to appreciate his wealth: They must see it for themselves.

It was for this reason he decided to have a new carriage built. He had seen carriages of other princes who ruled nearby kingdoms. Their carriages were much more lavish than his, which was now worn from years of travel. He realized his carriage could no longer be described as "fit for a prince."

His new carriage would be recognized as the most expensive in the land. It would include a diamond and emerald-studded hood and the finest silk draperies. Its seats would contain the softest leather. Its wheels would be constructed from the thickest iron in all the land.

Prince decided to announce his intention to replace their carriage while he and Cinderella rode to worship. The time alone, he felt, would enable him to fully describe each aspect of their new carriage. And so, clothed in their finery, he took her hand to help her into the carriage and he smiled broadly on this clear brisk morn. He felt sure that she would be exuberant and praise him for his modern ideas. Instead he heard her say in a troubled voice:

"Paying for such a carriage would require us to reduce our staff. We could no longer entertain our friends as frequently as we now do. And our diminished accounts would prohibit me from contributing funds for the new Food House. Besides, I would be embarrassed to ride in such an ostentatious carriage."

"Ostentatious?" Prince asked, confused, for he had seldom heard the word. "But a prince is supposed to have such a carriage! Besides, I have seen others ride in richly decorated carriages."

Cinderella spoke on and on, in a most disobedient manner. Prince hoped that the wind was sufficiently brisk to block her words from the coachman.

Finally, Prince interrupted, "Do you not understand that I am the Prince and you are the Prince's wife? Do you not understand that such a carriage befits our very status in this kingdom?"

Apparently, she did not understand. She repeated, in a variety of ways, what she had said before. Then she turned abruptly, grabbed embroidery from her basket, and began furiously attacking the stitching, as if she had to complete the piece before they arrived to greet the congregation.

Their dispute continued for weeks. He would explain why he must have such a carriage, and she would tell him that not only could they not afford such a purchase, but that it would make her uncomfortable to ride in a coach lavishly adorned with jewels.

Day after day they argued. Day after day, at work Prince had difficulty concentrating. At home, he slept fitfully, tossing so much that Cinderella frequented the guest chamber.

For weeks all he could visualize was the beauty of his new carriage and how he would supervise its construction. He imagined Cinderella finally agreeing that it was an excellent decision. He imagined himself holding her hand as she stepped from the coach and hearing the *ooohs* and *aaaahs* of the people. He smiled when he pictured the expression of Prince Showoffit, who currently owned the most elaborate of carriages.

One afternoon, Prince strolled from his office and took a bench beneath a chestnut tree. As he was eagerly devouring a chunk of spicy beef, still picturing his prize carriage, Caring Godfather sat down on the adjoining bench.

"So thy lady doth bother you once again."

"Indeed, and this time even *you* cannot aid me, for she misunderstands my princely purpose." Prince stared at the chestnuts that were scattered upon the ground.

Caring Godfather cleared his throat, but said no more.

"Cinderella and I cannot see eye to eye. I suspect our different upbringings are the cause."

"Your upbringings?"

"Oh, yes, I have told her many times that a new carriage is required and all she comprehends is that she will not have funds for entertaining friends and a Food House for the poor."

"So she wants thee not to have a carriage?"

"Perhaps she might allow a new carriage, but not one suitable for a prince. I suspect that grave differences in our upbringings are at fault. A suitable carriage for her is plain and drawn by a single brown horse. Perhaps our match was unsuitable," Prince said, lowering his head.

At this, Caring Godfather rose from his bench with some glee, his feet appearing to bounce to imaginary music as he floated a few inches from the soil.

"I think you understand very well, Prince. Very well, indeed!"

"How say you?" Prince asked.

"Well, thou say the dispute lies in the differences of what is right. It stems from what each has been taught. Thou must not be bound by thy earlier teachings. Instead, a new beginning is warranted of what is best, not for *thee*, nor *she*, but for *"we."*

*Thy goals and her desires point in different
directions,
The adverse results to both, are loss of your
affections;
A third approach from both of you is certainly
required,
To take this trip thou need to feel sufficiently
inspired.*

*Thy teachings from thy parents no longer fit thy
scheme,
Her teachings from her family obstruct thy
precious dream;
Do not maintain thy conventions that thou
learned in nursery,
Think "we" to set up new rules, for thy new
family!*

Caring Godfather quietly floated through the branches of the chestnut tree. Prince was left with a half-eaten meal and an empty stomach, but with a head full of ideas.

As he had done on previous occasions after Caring Godfather visited him, Prince called for his coachman to return him to the palace. When he arrived, he walked into a comical scene. Cinderella was supervising the palace repairmen, who were rebuilding the kitchen chimney. Pots and pans were in disarray on the kitchen floor and ashes were strewn helter-skelter. The workmen, as well as Cinderella, were covered with soot and the mess was so out of control that Cinderella and the workmen had no alternative but to be in a jovial mood.

As Prince walked in upon them, his belly rocked with laughter. Cinderella looked up at Prince and she, too, laughed uncontrollably. This was quite refreshing to both of them, considering their long-standing disagreement about the new carriage. Though she had never seen this part of his character, Prince began assisting the workmen as they removed the chimney bricks and she saw that he, too, was quickly as blackened as the others. Yet, Prince persisted until the work was complete.

Later, they called for their baths to be drawn. For the first time, they bathed together in the tub. Though Prince had been eager to speak with Cinderella of ways to compromise about the purchase of the carriage, it would have to await the proper time.

That eve as they dined, Prince told Cinderella that "to relieve our misery, it is desirable to think as '*we*.'"

And think they did.

"What, Cinderella, is your desire concerning a carriage?"

She hesitated, unsure whether he truly wished a response, but he nodded a few times, so she spoke directly. What she said made Prince feel that the two were again dancing at the ball:

"My dear, a new carriage is certainly essential. The old one is worn and needs swift replacement. 'Tis my desire that a new carriage be of the finest leather and be sufficiently large to carry the two of us and two others when required. It should be amply covered to protect us from the elements."

Prince nodded approvingly as she listed each requirement.

She continued: "And our current status should be considered. Sparkling glass, rather than jewels, should be at the fore to alert our citizens that the Prince arrives, but at an outlay within our means. What requirements do you believe are appropriate?"

Prince's face glowed. "Precisely as you have stated, with only two accompaniments. First, the glass should form a 'P & P' to announce that the Prince and Princess are in view. And second, a small chest should be attached in the rear for bread to offer to the poor and hungry."

Cinderella was so taken by this that she jumped up, knocking over her teacup and water goblet before hugging and kissing Prince with more passion than should have been witnessed by the servants in waiting.

Upon arriving at work the next day, Prince set out his inkwell and carefully penned:

Acceptance of Each Other's Values

*Think **We**, not you, nor me,*
*Think **We** for harmony;*
Do not maintain conventions we
  learned in nursery,
*Think **We** to establish rules for our*
  new family!

Months later, Prince and Cinderella saw a mare give birth to a new colt at dawn. She thought of a name for the colt, but decided to first ask Prince what name he thought appropriate. He responded, "Adam, since he is the first born of this mare." Then he added, "My lady, what do you wish?" She responded, "I was thinking of Boaz, which means swiftness in Hebrew." They finally chose "Abner," meaning the father of light, since the colt was born at sunrise. Over the months, asking and listening to each other in this way enabled them to make decisions which were better than either could make alone.

What Prince Learned About Differing Values

Early in their marriage, Prince believed his values were right and that before long he would convince Cinderella that his point of view made the most sense. Alas, he discovered that she thought her values made the most sense and, in time, he was sure to accept those values. They stood their ground and conflicts flared.

Prince, being reared in a royal household, was taught he must prove his importance by displaying his wealth. His father was forever trying to outshine the other kings with lavish displays of feasts and entertainment, by galloping the best horses throughout the kingdom and by dressing his footmen in red-velvet coats. Hence, Prince desired to own a lavish carriage. In contrast, Cinderella was taught by her mother that one should show consideration for others by being discreet in displaying even modest amounts of worldly goods.

As Prince and Cinderella began to understand their differences in upbringing, they realized why they were at odds deciding which carriage to acquire. Becoming more aware of the differences in values enabled them to avert future conflicts.

Prince penned three types of circumstances which might cause conflicts and how each should be handled:

First, were matters of importance to Cinderella, but of little importance to him. Such was the case with Cinderella's love of the palace pond. Because it was important to her that they maintain colorful fish and beautiful pond lilies, Prince supported her enthusiasm. In fact, he loved the idea that she found such enjoyment from its beauty, and he began to have greater appreciation for the pond.

Second, were matters of great interest to Prince, but of little interest to Cinderella. Such was Prince's love of jousting. Cinderella was never a great fan of the sport, but she learned to admire the skill and drama of jousting tournaments and often found herself caught up in Prince's enthusiasm.

Third, were the difficult situations when each felt quite strongly about an issue, such as the type of new carriage to acquire. In these situations, each understood that using only one of their values was not appropriate. Thus, a new way of thinking together and creating a new value was needed.

X

The Seventh Awareness
A Loving Relationship Requires Accepting and Being Grateful for Character Differences

NDERSTANDING different temperaments was a lesson Cinderella's mother never taught her. Alas, her mother died too soon.

"Why," she kept asking herself, "does Prince always arrive home later than he promises? Why is he not prompt? Why does he start a chore and complete it days or months later?" He would ask the masons to build a wall but not tell them where to acquire the stones. Months later, he would name the quarry and instruct them where to begin the wall but not tell them how far to extend it. Cinderella knew that one should be prompt and never fail to complete what one begins, or one should not begin at all.

It upset her to no end that Prince would not be ready when dinner guests arrived. Not only did he refuse to take heed of time schedules, but he made such light of it that she felt he mocked her for being prompt! After all, courtesy always requires promptness.

It came to pass that the King and Queen invited many guests to celebrate the one-year anniversary of Prince and Cinderella's nuptials. Judge and Mrs. Goodfellow were to attend. Dukes and duchesses and other royalty from all the land would attend. The most famous court jester would entertain them after they dined. Cinderella's stepmother and stepsisters would attend and require at least a few minutes to exchange pleasantries.

All was scheduled to begin at seven that eve. Cinderella ordered the four horses and carriage to be prepared at six for the hour's ride. She had a new gown sewn for the occasion and started to ready herself in the morn.

Prince promised to arrive home at four, but arrived at half-past five. Then he ordered a bath to be drawn.

"My dear!" Cinderella protested, "A bath you took this morn, and the appointed time at the King's palace is seven!"

Her pleas were to no avail, and they entered the carriage one-half hour late. Cinderella could no longer restrain herself and exclaimed to Prince that the King's dinner that eve *'twas in our own honour!* She stressed that many guests had come from afar and their dinner would be delayed due to Prince's "complete lack of consideration." Prince made no comment and even appeared to smile. They spoke not a word throughout the ride and arrived quite late.

Cinderella greeted the Queen with an embrace and a lowered head.

"What in heaven's name caused such delay?" the Queen asked. Neither replied. "The guests have been waiting. The King is quite upset and I was frightened that your carriage had fallen off the side of a cliff!"

"No, we are quite sound," Cinderella said sheepishly and looked across the room toward a musician who was strumming a harp.

After dinner, dancing and merriment ensued. Judge Goodfellow's toast reiterated the King and Queen's desire for progeny, which caused no end of laughter. The court jester's presentation was well received with amusement and standing applause. When the festivities ended, the carriage awaited them and Cinderella and Prince were no longer smiling.

"The evening was spoiled by your bath!" Cinderella said, folding her arms tightly and peering outside the carriage at a moonless night.

"On the contrary, the evening was spoiled by your adverse attitude. Neither guests nor the King were bothered by the short delay."

They spoke no more and later lay in bed, back to back. Neither slept well. Even until the next morn, not a word transpired.

By late afternoon, while Prince was at work, Cinderella had lost all vigor and lay down to rest. She dreamt of trying to leave the ballroom as the clock struck twelve. In her dream, the gown Fairy Godmother had bestowed upon her had already turned to rags. The palace guards were rushing toward her, but her feet thrust forward not making traction. The guards drew near, reaching out to grasp her!

When she awoke she felt moisture on her pillow from her tears and saw that Fairy Godmother had already entered the room through the window.

"Well, Cinderella, it seems that you and Prince have not been seeing eye to eye, nor hearing mouth to ear," Fairy Godmother said.

"Oh, it has been so terrible! Prince never seems to keep on schedule and it causes me much embarrassment. Also, it takes him many moons to finish any castle work."

"Hmmm," Fairy Godmother said, noticing that tears filled Cinderella's eyes.

"If only he would be as I, and be prompt. If only he would finish work at home swiftly!"

Again Fairy Godmother said, "Hmmm."

"Perhaps I should not have chosen a prince. Another might have suited me better. Someone who acts more as I."

"Well, temperaments do vary from one to another. There are great varieties, and in marriage the heavens doth not seek to match those who possess the same, for it doesn't serve a couple well. What is best to understand is":

The way in which we do engage,
Begins at birth and does not change;

Some are flexible and always relax,
Others think time should be sharp as an axe;

Each is quite right in his own perspective,
Though the other fails to see his objective;

To resolve confusion between you two,
Requires accepting each other's view.

As soon as these last words were spoken, Cinderella saw Fairy Godmother fly directly out through the window, though she knew not how, since the window was firmly closed. Cinderella's eyes now saw clearly, and her mind was able to focus on Fairy Godmother's words. So, if there is no way to alter Prince's temperament, how then could they engage happily? Fairy Godmother says the heavens do not seek a match in temperament. She wondered how it would be if Prince and she agreed on everything, and she felt a dullness settle in.

She loved his great spirit and energy, even when it was accompanied by disorder and confusion; yet, she also knew she could not again bear the humiliation of arriving late for a festival in *their* honour. What a dilemma! Why hadn't Fairy Godmother explained more?

In this state, she wandered into the palace library looking for answers. She flipped through a number of dusty books but found none concerning temperament. Then she was taken by a volume written by Aristotle and one by Plato.

Hidden within their philosophy lessons, they described how the temperament of individuals differ and each type is beneficial in different ways. Some are quite analytical and devote much energy to solving problems, whereas others are more conscious of a person's emotions. Some are enormously creative and look at future possibilities, while others are practical and deal with the here and now. She thought of Prince. True, he was often late and frequently began a palace project only to finish it many months later. But Prince was flexible and could easily adjust to new situations, such as changing his jousting schedule so promptly.

She loved his enthusiasm and exciting ideas. He always managed to find a spectacularly beautiful picnic location. When they dined, she felt his eagerness to discuss the day's exciting events. Many evenings, he surprised her with a bouquet of daffodils. Cinderella realized that her methods were more practical, more useful, in contrast to Prince's exceptionally wild ideas.

Flashing in Cinderella's mind were the words: *All the joy and excitement he brings to me, I must not lose.*

After dinner, she requested a special conversation with Prince. At first he was reluctant, complaining that he must exercise to prepare his muscles for the jousting match, but she persisted and he relented.

They walked into the garden and seated themselves on a bench near the fish pond.

"Dear," she began. "I want to tell you how much I enjoy

your demeanor. I love your exuberance and your ability to change plans to adjust to any situation. You surprise me in selecting beautiful places to picnic and interesting paths to ride our horses. You express such energy whenever we entertain guests."

Prince smiled. He drummed his fingers against the iron bench, knowing that Cinderella was going to insert an enormous *HOWEVER,* and surely she did:

"However, my dearest, when the King and Queen held the celebration for our one-year anniversary and we arrived half past the appointed hour, my knees almost fell me to the ground with embarrassment."

Prince bit his lower lip. He heard Caring Godfather's voice repeating, "True love requires accepting all feelings....True love requires acceptance...." Prince knew his feelings were contrary to Cinderella's, for only the Queen had expressed an objection to the delay. Just the same, his lady was greatly bothered and Caring Godfather had taught him to accept her emotions, even if his feelings differed.

And so he told his love:

"My dear, I fully understand that it caused you great distress, though I was not bothered by our late arrival. To set things right in the future, pray tell me when I cause such stress. I vow that I shall listen and act to ease your feelings."

Cinderella threw her arms around him and Prince held her very tight. Her warm body and sweet womanly scent made him wish never to release her. Then she whispered into his ear, "My darling, as you know, you never need be as I, nor I as you. The greater beauty grows as we entwine two spirits."

Prince whispered back, "And your exquisite spirit will forever be entwined with mine."

The next day Cinderella wrote the following and placed the parchment where she had placed the others:

Accepting and Being Grateful for Character Differences

This I will accept to live cheerfully:
Temperaments will vary between him
& me.
'Tis smart to remember, 'tis heaven's
design,
For two special temperaments make our
day shine.

What Cinderella Learned About Character Differences

Cinderella realized that she and Prince had major character differences which caused distress. She also knew their basic personalities were not likely to change. However, over time they learned to use these differences to create a unique energy that deepened their love. They found that, just as a fire safely burning in a fireplace warms the soul, the proper use and acceptance of varying temperaments would keep their flame alive, bright, and under control.

Cinderella contemplated each of their character differences:

First, she was more social and felt energized in the company of friends. She loved conversing with others, and conducting meetings to plan help for the poor. Prince, on the other hand, needed many hours of private time. He was content to return from work and study at length in his library. At afternoon tea, he enjoyed speaking with Cinderella of the theories of ancient philosophers. He also spent considerable time alone planning his tactics for the next jousting match.

Second, Prince was more creative and Cinderella was more practical. He found ways for his workmen to dig new carriage roads so storms would not wash them away. He invented an echo passageway in a downstairs closet of their palace so he could call to Cinderella when she was in the upstairs hallway.

He loved to focus on possibilities for the future. He spoke of a time when information could be transmitted faster than any stallion could gallop. He believed that in the future there would be some sort of contraption that would plant seeds and harvest, instead of a farmer and his mule doing this work. She loved his romantic ways. She was tickled whenever he serenaded her with open arms as he descended the staircase afore dinner. She was enthralled when he entertained her with his wild stories.

Cinderella tended to concentrate more on the here and now. She efficiently managed the entire palace staff, providing a comfortable life for all. She oversaw the garden, knowing that her flowers would not grow if not properly planted and maintained. She planned for food to be delivered daily to the poor houses. Through it all, she encouraged Prince to share his dreams and fantasies, while he learned to appreciate her practical approach of getting work done in an efficient and timely manner.

Third, Cinderella could better understand another's true feelings. When the Queen made a statement, Cinderella was able to discern her true meaning by searching her face and posture. Prince might remember each word, but he had difficulty discovering hidden emotions. When it came to analyzing available facts, Prince was king! He reviewed them and re-reviewed them. He could determine exactly how many bushels of wheat could be grown on 36 acres, when the plot lay near a river. He could calculate the speeds of five stallions in a race.

Fourth, Cinderella was always punctual, whereas Prince was oblivious to time schedules. When a servant resigned from palace work, she knew it was her job to hire a replacement, for it would have taken Prince many moons to do so. A schedule for Prince was only a guide and was frequently altered, even if the schedule was set by others. Hence, it was not important for him to arrive at the Queen's party at seven in the eve, nor did it matter if he began a new task before completing a prior one. Consistent with her desire for completion, Cinderella would finish each task she began.

Over time they learned to admire each other's ways and found that diversity added spice and spirit to their relationship. When a conflict ensued they listened intently and learned to understand each other's perspective. They found there is no right or wrong, just a different way of viewing the world. Only then is compromise possible. Prince realized that it is crucial for Cinderella to be on time for important events so he made every effort to be

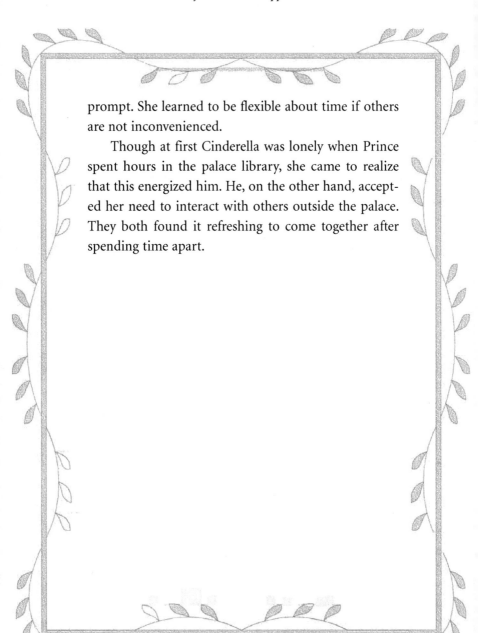

prompt. She learned to be flexible about time if others are not inconvenienced.

Though at first Cinderella was lonely when Prince spent hours in the palace library, she came to realize that this energized him. He, on the other hand, accepted her need to interact with others outside the palace. They both found it refreshing to come together after spending time apart.

XI
The Eighth Awareness
A Loving Relationship Requires
An Equal Partnership

VER TIME, Cinderella made more and more decisions on her own. Prince became quite uneasy with her independent behavior. He is a prince, and she had been a commoner. It was improper for her to carry on with such independence. She established the Food House in the village square and then, without consulting Prince, doubled the House's size when the adjacent building was available. Now, he heard, she was adding *area* Food Houses beyond the village hills and helping to manage all of them.

Even worse was her new endeavor: She would ride her favourite mare to the village and meet with small groups of citizens. At these gatherings she would ask, "Pray tell, in what ways can the kingdom provide you with greater happiness?" *Heresy!* was what he heard one knight voice to another. *Heresy!*

When Prince toured the village he found drawings of Cinderella posted in the village square. Below each were written superlatives such as: *Our Shining Princess!* and *Our Princess Who Cares for All the Kingdom's Citizens!*

Prince was quite distraught. My citizens say she cares, but they say nothing of me? Why is it her image, not mine, that is posted in the village, after all I have done to build their roads, to protect them with my knights, and even to entertain them by conveying jesters to the village square?

It did not fit his sense of propriety that a woman, especially his wife, should take such action. A princess talking directly to the people? *'Twas heresy!*

It was so unfair that her image was posted in the village. Women, as everyone knew, must not involve themselves with such activities outside the home. If all the wives left their homes in such a manner, who would care for the young? Who would assure that the bread sat upon the table?

Prince began to doubt his princely power. Though he made scores of pronouncements and the King had honoured all but a few, he was anguished when the King overruled him. To add to his woes, he no longer felt he had full command of his life at home. His wife, whom he selected when she was a commoner, was now encroaching on his lordly power! Yes, he must nip the Cinderella problem in the bud!

Days earlier, he practiced what he would say to her. He would be straightforth:

"Cinderella," he would say, "Cinderella, I can no longer allow your outrageous behaviour. Your actions encourage citizens to disrespect the royal family. It is improper for you to ask our citizens what they need from us. We are the royal family, and we decide what is required to run this kingdom. 'Tis heresy to do otherwise!"

Yes, that is what he would tell Cinderella, and she would cease and desist immediately from meeting with the citizens. With that in mind, after dinner Prince approached Cinderella in the parlour. She brushed a wisp of hair from her forehead and smiled her warm smile as they sat down.

"Cinderella," he began, using the most authoritative voice he could muster, "Cinderella, I wish to discuss your present activities in feeding the poor and talking with citizens."

"Oh, Prince," she said, "I've wanted to do so with you. I am so grateful for this opportunity. The poor certainly need more food and our citizens have fine ideas that cost little and will—"

"Cinderella, I am not talking about their needs. I am talking about your inappropriate actions to overrule the Crown!"

"But, dear, some need more aid. They certainly are suffering and it is imperative that they tell us how they-"

Prince stood up and raised his chin toward her. He felt his blood boiling. He wiped sweat from his brow. He could no longer contain himself. He pointed his finger across the table: "Cinderella, I warn you! You must not enhance this program. The King and I direct our kingdom. I forbid you to further converse with my citizens!"

She had never heard Prince speak this way. It was a foreign tongue to her ears. His voice echoed her stepmother's when she had first ordered Cinderella to sleep on straw near the attic stairs.

As he pointed at her, she could no longer withhold her tears, which flowed freely. She covered her face and turned toward the fireplace. With that, Prince shouted: "I am the Prince and will not stand for this!" He stomped out of the parlour. She heard his feet hit each stair before the outside door of the palace slammed. Peeking through the curtains, she saw him saddle up his stallion and gallop off.

They did not speak that evening, nor in the morn, nor the whole next day, nor the following day. They took separate meals and slept apart.

Three days later, Prince sat in his office, still troubled. His thoughts swung from anger, as he thought of her terrible deeds, to a broken heart, as he pictured the warmth and love that she now held in reserve.

His own words haunted him. He remembered his sharp tongue as though it was a wolfhound's bark. The blood flowed into his cheeks with shame when he remembered himself saying, "Cinderella, I warn you!" They were words he once heard the King blare at the Queen when Prince was a child. He remembered how he had run from their battle into the palace basement and played with a toy soldier in the dark.

Totally confused as to what to do now, Prince held his forehead in the palm of his hand. He discovered tears running down one cheek. This both relieved his tension, yet puzzled him because he could not recall feeling his own tears except when he was young and had fallen from a pony. It was the time the King had shrieked at him: "A prince does not cry!" No tears had been shed since.

"Ahem," Caring Godfather said, appearing nearby in a chair. "Ahem."

Prince failed to raise his eyes but spoke: "'Tis quite unfair, Caring Godfather. 'Tis quite unfair that a prince gains less respect from his citizens than doth his lady. The King and I have aided the citizens for many long years, as did my grandfather and his father, afore. Now Cinderella merely listens to them talk and they are grateful unto her."

Caring Godfather waited a long time, using the power of silence to calm Prince's emotions. Finally, Prince released his palm from his forehead and looked up at Caring Godfather.

"My dear Prince," Caring Godfather began, "I see you have respect and love for your citizens."

"Oh, yes, I have great love for them and I truly respect their abilities. They try hard to support themselves and to support the Crown."

"I see…. But thou believest Cinderella gives the poor too much?"

Prince had not thought about whether Cinderella was giving too much food to the poor or too much housing for the homeless, but he did feel her to be too friendly with the common people.

"Well, Caring Godfather, I am upset that she gets so involved and asks them what would generate happiness for themselves. It certainly is the King's duty to decide such matters."

"And the King knows what would make the citizens happy?"

"Well, he should. He should, for he is the King," Prince said, meekly, for he wasn't quite sure whether the King did know. When Prince was young, the King certainly did not understand Prince's desires.

"Well, sometimes, it is difficult for one to know what another thinks and feels. Even the King might have difficulty reading another's mind."

Prince felt as though Caring Godfather was twisting his thoughts. However, Caring Godfather had always helped in the past, so he was eager to receive advice.

"You see," Caring Godfather continued, "methinks thy lady's fame has upset thee. Perhaps, Prince, thou are not so distraught by thy lady's purpose in helping, but by the popularity she gains by talking directly with the commoners."

"You suggest," Prince said, "that I am jealous of her popularity? I, the Prince, would worry about remarks of the common citizens?"

"Doth thee not have a feeling soul?" Caring Godfather asked.

Prince sat quietly.

"This is what should set you straight:"

Methinks that Cinderella's fame,
Brings discomfort and your shame;

I know it generates many fears,
When common people offer ideas;
This practice reverses the norms of the nation:
Ideas that come from lesser stations;

Rather than telling thy lady to suppress,
You should join her newfound happiness;
Though at times one partner feels finer,
Love can't survive with one major and one minor;

So arm in arm, with thy lady you should go,
And find both thy marriage and kingdom grow!

As Caring Godfather rose effortlessly and retreated, Prince's despondency followed suit. However, Prince knew it would take a great effort to join Cinderella's cause, for he had never before asked citizens for their thoughts. Besides, after insulting his lady, how could he now approach her as Caring Godfather suggested?

Prince realized that the courage required when jousting

was as small as a ladybug compared with the courage required to confess his errors to his lady. But as the Prince of the kingdom and as the Commander of the Circle of Knights, duty called him to undertake this mission.

And so he did. With only a slight crack in his voice and a well-rehearsed tongue, he explained:

"Cinderella, I have conversed at length with the heavens. My decision has been made. My King has always commanded the citizens and never requested their opinions. But to meet with new ways, required of new times, I can no longer agree with the King. I will join with my lady's view of full discussion with my citizens. However, the King is still the King and I must have a tête-à-tête with him about this issue."

Cinderella's eyes filled with tears. She appeared more dear than when he had first greeted her at the ball. She could not and did not wish to contain her excitement. Bounding from her chair, she again splashed her teacup, and threw her arms around Prince's muscular frame.

The next day Prince placed the following in his *IMPORTANT PARCHMENTS* cabinet:

True Love Requires Equality

Then he drew out his finest goose quill and wrote:

An important note to the King:

Sir, I have a matter of utmost urgency that I must discuss with you. It would please me if I could meet with you tomorrow morn.

Prince

In the past, Prince had made proposals to the King which were either accepted or rejected with little discussion. But this time he had some doubt as to whether the King would acquiesce. He also knew that he must press his point because of his strong belief that it was the right thing to do for the citizens of the kingdom, and because of his promise to Cinderella. Yes, he must finally stand up to his father who continued to control the purse strings. With these thoughts, he called for his page to deliver his note to the King.

Prince Learned That True Love Requires An Equal Partner

At the time of his wedding, Prince knew that the man should be head of the household. All the men he spoke with felt the same. However, in the months thereafter, he realized that such a belief was outdated and anchored for millenniums only through men's muscles. Actually, women frequently outwitted men while allowing them to maintain control.

But how could a couple live joyfully, side-by-side, if each continually sought ways to control the other? Even if he knew that his decisions would rule, was this worth the pain he and Cinderella endured over the months? Luckily, Prince learned early in his marriage that equal consideration and respect for each other's needs and abilities was essential for them to live happily ever after. To do otherwise meant recurrent battles in the royal household.

True, Prince was superior in many ways. He could gallop on his stallion much faster. He was endowed with stronger muscles, so he could carry heavier loads and run faster. He was also quicker in mathematical calculations and could remember places and roads as if they were drawn in his brain.

But, oh! Cinderella's virtues went far beyond her kindness and beauty. Her sense of what was needed to help all the citizens of the kingdom amazed Prince. As she conversed with others, her intuitiveness was exceptionally keen, enabling her to communicate with the lords and ladies as well as the populace of all ranks. She also read faster than Prince, and he sometimes had to ask for assistance in determining the meaning of a passage in a book.

Prince discovered that equality did not mean being equal in all abilities, but it did show that each must treat the other as equal in stature. With all his heart Prince now understood that his marriage to Cinderella was an equal partnership, regardless of tradition or the King and Queen's views.

XII

Full Awareness
A Loving Relationship Requires
Understanding and Using All
Eight Awarenesses

HE next morn Prince took his breakfast early with Cinderella and spoke with glee about how he would explain to the King exactly what is needed to improve relationships with the citizens. She smiled when he said he would not ask, but tell the King, that the kingdom must move ahead with newfound energy and the only way, yes, the *only* way this could happen is to involve the citizenry with major decisions that impact their lives. Citizens must be given an opportunity to comment before final decisions are made by the King and the Prince. The people must be able to comment before roads are built, before armies are raised, before land is assigned to farmers or dukes or duchesses.

Cinderella smiled as the strength of Prince's voice rose to

support her ideals. She could not contain herself, and wished to shout, "Yes! Yes! That is exactly what I have been telling you!" but she remained composed. As Prince entered his carriage, she wished him good luck and kissed him adieu.

Throughout the carriage ride, his thoughts of how he would dazzle the King remained with him. When he entered the palace, the Prince's personal page greeted him with these words:

"Sir, the King must see you immediately!"

The page then drew close and whispered, "It seems the King's disposition is more troubling than a wild boar trapped in the stables." The page walked quickly away from Prince, down the marble hall. Prince walked slowly, in the opposite direction, toward the King's office, massaging the back of his neck. When he entered the outer office, an attending knight told him the King was occupied. Prince busied himself with a document from his satchel, reading the document several times before realizing that his mind paid no attention to the words. He seemed to remain there forever, but it may only have been the time it took for a horse to be saddled.

As he was finally shown in, he faced a King with folded arms. The King motioned for Prince to sit in a chair directly in front of his work table.

" Good morning," Prince said, hearing the words crack in his throat.

The King was silent for quite some time. Finally, he said,

"Cinderella!" The name echoed in the chamber. The King pursed his lips, his fist pushing up his chin.

"Yes?" Prince said, glancing at the parchments on the King's work table to avoid his penetrating eyes.

"Your wife, Cinderella!" the King said, awaiting some kind of response, but Prince knew not what to say.

The King continued, "Your wife, Cinderella, who has started food banks and homeless shelters has now gone further than any woman should journey into the affairs of the Crown!"

The sound of his father's voice reminded Prince of the many times he had heard his father use this tone to attack his mother or himself. In Prince's mind's eye, a picture flashed of his father screaming at him when he failed to gather himself from the mud after tumbling off his first full-size stallion. Stable hands had seen him fall, and the King's crimson face had glanced down at Prince and then to the stable hands who had burst into laughter. Prince had finally pried himself from the mud and run into the palace, hiding for hours in a room off the pantry until the King retired for the night. In the morn the King said not a word, simply turning his head from side to side as he walked past Prince.

Now, as he sat before the King, Prince's belly throbbed and he wished there was a way to retreat into his own office.

"Your wife, Cinderella, is now asking *my* populace to tell her what they desire! My knights have told me this directly! She has asked *my* populace what they want from the King!"

Prince sat in the chair, tapping his foot on the marble slab. He could no longer allow the King to belittle him. He remembered that he, Prince, was captain of the jousting team. He was the man who would one day be King and he had to defend his wife, and his future kingdom, from the wrath of this wild boar!

The anger in Prince's heart matched that of the King's. Prince rose from the chair, and in a controlled forceful voice, said: "Father, your ideas are being left behind! Kings have fallen in the past and will continue to fall unless changes are made. We must begin immediately to govern differently, as I will do when I am King! Yes, Cinderella is asking our citizens what they need because we have failed to do so. You have ignored the rights of our citizens. Maybe she should have consulted you, but I can tell by your present demeanor what results would have followed if she had."

Suddenly, the King rose from his chair and pointed his finger at Prince's head. "Your obstreperous behavior is completely inappropriate and I will not stand for it! I am still King and have always considered the populace in my edicts. I would gladly compare my generosity to any king in the land!"

Prince could no longer stand there as the King pointed. He drew his hand into the air and pointed even more forcefully at the King, "Our citizens deserve more than the mere tokens you occasionally deign to bestow on them. Citizens have a right to speak up for their desires and needs. You, sir, will never survive your tenure unless my ideas and Cinderella's are incorporated into our kingdom! Good-day, sir!"

And with that, Prince lifted his chin toward the King, turned, and walked briskly out of the chamber.

*   *   *

Prince returned from work and told Cinderella in detail what had transpired in the King's office. As she listened, Cinderella kept repeating, "Oh, my! Oh, my!" But when he had completed his tale, she rushed over and threw her arms around him and told him how very proud indeed she was of his courage.

There was silence between the King and Prince for eleven days. And on the twelfth day, a messenger galloped to Prince and Cinderella's palace to deliver a scroll. When Prince broke the Queen's seal he read:

> My Dear Prince and Cinderella,
>
> Your father and I wish for you both to dine with us privately tomorrow eve at the hour of six. Your father has been much distraught for these many days and nights and wishes for all of us to use a civil tongue and confer about the matter you have previously discussed.
>
> > Our love to you both,
> > Mother

*   *   *

For the first time, Prince was waiting for their carriage even before Cinderella finished dressing. If the Queen said the hour of six, Prince would arrive not a moment later. During the ride to the King's palace, they speculated as to what the King might say. Prince was sure his father would not budge from his former position. Cinderella said she surely hoped the King would at least provide their citizens some voice on how they were to be governed.

An hour later the four of them sat at dinner while servants adorned their plates with duckling and squash and filled their goblets with burgundy. The Queen and Cinderella chatted on with glee about their gardens and the new fashions introduced by some of the duchesses in nearby kingdoms. Much of the time the King and Prince were silent and listened to the women. When the men talked, it was about the weather and the speed of their horses, with nary a smile exhibited by either.

After the plum pudding was consumed, the Queen suggested they adjourn to the parlour. Cinderella and Prince eagerly waited for the King to speak about the subject that was forbidden during dinner.

The King began: "Prince, regarding our last exchange of words, I wish to make myself totally clear. My ideas are completely different from—"

"Well, your ideas are certainly not—" Prince began, but Cinderella touched him on the shoulder, turned toward the

King and said, "So, Sir, you are saying that your ideas are completely different?"

"Yes," the King continued, "I believe that it is not appropriate for you, Cinderella, to approach my populace and ask them for their ideas."

Cinderella nodded and said, "So you feel I should not be asking the citizens for their ideas."

"Definitely! Absolutely not! So I see you understand me."

At this, Prince again began to speak but Cinderella again tapped his arm.

"Yes," the King continued, " What I wish to do is to issue a proclamation to the pop – er, citizens. I wish to meet with them with the four of us in attendance. We will request their ideas as to what actions should be taken in the kingdom that would please them. Yes, and I have decided this meeting will occur only on the first day of September, each year."

The King's gentle smile was caught by the Queen who sought a reciprocal smile from Prince and Cinderella.

Prince and Cinderella sat there stunned. Here was the King proposing the change that they believed could never occur. It wasn't exactly what they would have done, but it was a major transformation in the King's philosophy. Prince clasped Cinderella's hand and they both smiled broadly. Cinderella looked up to meet the Queen's eyes and understood the Queen was offering the warmth of bonding, without words, that women can understand much better than men.

Traveling home, Prince realized that the King's acceptance of Cinderella's dream would allow the people of the kingdom to participate in major decisions and would set the stage for him when he became King. And it also revealed to Prince that his marriage would remain harmonious and joyful only if Cinderella and he each felt there was equality in thoughts and deeds. As they rode home, they talked at length about the changes that were to occur and were surprised how fast the coachman delivered them.

*   *   *

The following day Cinderella planned a picnic. She decided this was the ideal time to present Prince with each of the parchments hidden with her personal belongings. After all, she reasoned, it is to the advantage of both that they follow Fairy Godmother's advice.

After they began their journey, Prince instructed the coachman to transport them to the King's palace. Upon arriving, he bid Cinderella to join him in his office chamber.

"My dear," he said, "I must confess to thee that over the months, I have received assistance on the means to resolve our quarrels." He unlocked his cabinet marked **IMPORTANT PARCHMENTS** and withdrew the four scrolls. "This support was provided by my Caring Godfather whose advice has served us well."

Cinderella smiled more broadly than at any time he had known her. He unrolled his parchments and displayed them before her eyes. Cinderella then reached into the picnic basket she was carrying and withdrew the four parchments she had hidden beside the food.

"My dear Prince, I too, must confess that I have received the advice of my Fairy Godmother. Without her wise words, our disagreements could never have been resolved." As she unveiled her parchments, the two broke into uncontrollable laughter, with Cinderella pulling Prince tight and snuggling her head onto his shoulder.

After several moments Cinderella and Prince sat down admiring the eight parchments. They realized the parchments fit so well in tone that they should blend them into a single document.

Full Awareness
A Loving Relationship Requires:

First Awareness
> *Daily Appreciations*

Second Awareness
> *Accepting Each Other's Perspective and Feelings*

Third Awareness
> *Supporting Each Other When Relatives Interfere*

Fourth Awareness
Togetherness
Fifth Awareness
Physical Intimacy
Sixth Awareness
Accepting Each Other's Different Values
Seventh Awareness
Accepting and Being Grateful for Character Differences
Eighth Awareness
An Equal Partnership

After merging their parchments, Prince took Cinderella's hand and they strolled to the old chestnut tree to picnic. When they finished their Yorkshire pudding and roasted chicken, they began to devour cherry pie with tea. At that moment, they saw Fairy Godmother and Caring Godfather floating toward them, both with smiles as broad as the chestnut tree. Caring Godfather spoke: "We have come to say *good-day* and we have come to say *adieu.*"

Both Cinderella and Prince were astonished. Prince had never seen Fairy Godmother, nor had Cinderella seen Caring Godfather. Usually, their godparents arrived alone, and only when they faced a dilemma.

"Yes," said Fairy Godmother, "We see that both of you

now understand our eight teachings. This is what is needed to live happily ever after. You no longer require our help."

Caring Godfather and Fairy Godmother smiled down upon the couple. Fairy Godmother then said:

At the wondrous ball, together you found,
Love and ecstasy, and you were spellbound;
Now you've learned lasting love requires,
Awareness of each other's needs and desires.

Though you'll oft feel great pleasure and you'll oft
*   be inspired,*
Life is ne'er perfect, so vigilance is required;
I warned Cinderella of the midnight hour,
Now I must caution you: Your bond needs
*   willpower;*

So continue to note your special differences,
Don't push your beliefs on your Mister or Missus;
Through Full Awareness, your conflicts are less,
And you'll delight each other, with minimal
*   distress.*

Then Caring Godfather spoke to the couple. "Remember":

The one true happiness on this earth or above,
Is to be loved by another and have someone to love;
Kings, o'er the ages, hoarded gold and much more,
But most would trade all for the one they'd adore!

Cinderella and Prince gazed at their godparents floating higher and higher, disappearing through the chestnut tree. They were not sure they would ever see them again, but they knew they would always remember their godparents.

After their carriage returned them to the palace, Cinderella reached into her armoire. She found the single glass slipper that she had lost while running from the ball, the one Prince had retrieved. She beckoned to Prince to join her upstairs. He bounded the stairs and she met him at the landing. Cinderella extended her arm to display the slipper. Silently, they gazed into the sparkling glass. It reflected the same joy they had felt on their honeymoon — that experience when love was tender and unconditional, when trust was full, and when each was the other's best friend.

They looked upon their future together, but now they could see a profound difference in their reflection from the year past. There was a new dimension: that of awareness and understanding. They realized that what they now saw in the glass slipper were the changes each had made to deepen their love. They knew that disagreements would occur, but through their conscious relationship they could use the eight awarenesses to resolve the issues. They also knew their happiness together would continue on earth and in the heavens forever and ever after.

XIII
Epilogue

NE MONTH later Prince announced to the kingdom that Cinderella was with child.

Thus began preparations for the celebration of the royal birth. Awaiting this child created even greater love for each other.

Their marriage, however, was not without conflicts. As with all relationships, differences arose over the years, along with great joy, harmony, and love. Their Full Awareness served them well. They always knew that they could depend on an Awareness to resolve any issue, no matter how troublesome. They noticed more and more that their differences could increase the excitement in their lives just as spices added flavour to their favourite cuisine. At the same time their conflicts lessened, and the stress they had felt in their earlier months of marriage was greatly diminished.

Yes, Cinderella and Prince lived happily ever after, with a deep love that would serve as a model for their children and their children's children.

XIV
The History of Cinderella

INDERELLA is one of the most recognized stories. There are over 1,000 versions and almost every country in the world has developed a Cinderella story.

The tale is based on a young lady, Cinderella, who is both kind and beautiful, whose father remarries after his wife dies. Cinderella is treated dreadfully by her stepmother and her two stepsisters. In some versions, her father is absent; in others he allows his new wife to rule the household and control his daughter.

The earliest version of *Cinderella* was written in China in the 9th century by Tuan Ch'eng-shih, but even his written tale was based on folklore that may have been told for hundreds of years. *Cinderella*, written by Frenchman Charles Perrault in 1697, is the basis for most of the present day Cinderella stories; it included the fairy godmother character, replacing the magical fish of the Chinese story. Charles

Perrault's tale has Cinderella forgiving and finding husbands for her wicked stepsisters.

In modern times, the Cinderella tale has been retold in books, movies, novels, and musicals. In all versions, the story has ended with Cinderella and the Prince marrying and implying, if not actually stating, *they lived happily every after.* In the original 1950 Walt Disney movie version, these were the last words on the screen.

About the Authors

Jon Meyerson is a licensed clinical social worker and his wife **Beverly Meyerson** is a relational coach. The Meyersons have coached hundreds of couples in their Bethesda, Maryland and Sarasota, Florida offices, where they teach the concept of full awareness. They also practice full awareness daily in their personal lives.

To purchase additional copies of *After the Glass Slipper*

♦ Order from your local bookstore, Amazon.com, BarnesAndNoble.com or other on-line store.

♦ On-line book stores in foreign countries include: Amazon.co.uk (England) BoomarangBooks.com (Australia)

♦ Contact us through www.AfterTheGlassSlipper.com for discounts on bulk orders, autographed copies and international delivery.

♦ We welcome comments, endorsements, or questions. www.AfterTheGlassSlipper.com

Breinigsville, PA USA
22 September 2010
245856BV00001B/331/P